This Topsy and Tim book belongs to

Raymond Chen

All Ladybird books are available at most bookshops, supermarkets
and newsagents, or can be ordered direct from:
Ladybird Postal Sales PO Box 133 Paignton TQ3 2YP England
Telephone: (+44) 01803 554761   *Fax:* (+44) 01803 663394
A catalogue record for this book is available from the British Library

Published by Ladybird Books Ltd
A subsidiary of the Penguin Group
A Pearson Company

© Jean and Gareth Adamson MCMXCV
This edition MCMXCIX

The moral rights of the author/illustrator have been asserted
LADYBIRD and the device of a Ladybird are trademarks of Ladybird Books Ltd Loughborough Leicestershire UK

Topsy + Tim

growing up stories

Jean and Gareth Adamson

Ladybird

Contents

Topsy +Tim

go on an aeroplane

Topsy and Tim were off on their
summer holidays. They were going
in an aeroplane.

The airport was very big.
Topsy and Tim had a long ride in a bus
to reach the terminal building.

Then they had a long ride on an escalator to get to the right part of the building.

Their luggage went for a long ride too, on a moving platform.

Topsy and Tim watched an aeroplane land.
It looked much bigger when it was
not in the sky.

The door was high off the ground.
'How will the people get out?'
asked Topsy.

'Through a special tunnel,'
said Mummy. 'You will see when
it's our turn to get on the plane.'

The loudspeaker voice announced
that Topsy and Tim's aeroplane
was ready. Soon they were walking along
a telescopic tunnel and stepping
into the aeroplane. It looked like
a very long bus.

'Welcome aboard,' said the stewardess
to Topsy and Tim.

The stewardess helped Topsy and Tim
fasten their safety belts.
She gave them some comics
and some sweets.

'Suck a sweet when the aeroplane
starts to fly,' she said. 'It will
stop your ears hurting.
Tim took two sweets.
'One for each ear,' he said.
The stewardess laughed.
'They go in your mouth,
not your ears!' she said.

The big aeroplane flew up into the sky.
Topsy and Tim watched trees and houses
grow as small as toys.
'My ears have gone funny,' said Topsy.
'You didn't suck your sweet, that's why,'
said Tim.

Topsy and Tim were flying above the clouds.
'Isn't this exciting!' said Mummy.
But the clouds went on for miles and miles.
Topsy and Tim began to fidget.

Lunch came in interesting plastic trays.
Each piece of food had its own
shaped space, like the pieces
of a jigsaw puzzle. Topsy and Tim
tried to swop pieces. The stewardess
had to clear up the mess.
Then she said, 'Topsy and Tim,
the pilot would like to talk to you.'

The stewardess took Topsy and Tim
to the pilot's cabin.
'Hello twins,' said the pilot.
'I've been hearing about you.'
He showed Topsy and Tim all the
switches and levers and dials
he used to fly the aeroplane.
'Do you think you could fly
my aeroplane?' asked the pilot.
Topsy and Tim were not sure.

They went back to their seats and
fastened their safety belts once more.
Then they pretended to be pilots.
'Will you land our aeroplane now,
please, pilots?' asked the stewardess.

Topsy and Tim could see the flaps
moving in the aeroplane's wings
to make it fly lower.
'I'm doing that when I move this lever,'
said Tim. But Topsy and Tim both knew
the real pilot was doing it.

Topsy and Tim's aeroplane landed
with hardly a bump.

'Goodbye everybody,' said Topsy and Tim. They waved goodbye to the stewardess and to the pilot up in the aeroplane's nose. Then they went to meet their luggage on another moving platform.

And that is how Topsy and Tim flew in an aeroplane.

Topsy + Tim

go on a train

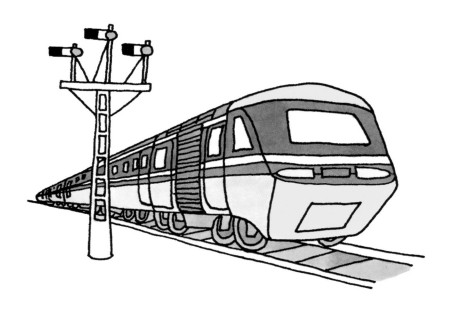

Topsy and Tim were going to visit
their granny. They were going by
train because Granny lived a long
way away.
'Hurry up, Topsy and Tim,' said
Mummy. 'We mustn't miss our train.'

They were taking a lot of luggage
with them, so Mummy called a taxi
to drive them to the station.
'I wish we could go faster,' said
Tim. 'We'll miss the train.'
'No, we won't,' said Mummy.

They reached the station with
plenty of time to spare.

The kind taxi driver found a
special trolley for the luggage.
Topsy and Tim helped push it
through the booking hall.

People were queuing to buy tickets
at the ticket office.
'I'm glad I came to buy our tickets
yesterday,' said Mummy. 'Now we
don't have to join that queue.'

'Our train leaves from Platform 2,'
said Mummy. She showed their tickets
to the platform guard.
'Platform 2 is over the bridge,' he
told them.

'Phew!' said Tim as they pushed their trolley up the slope to the bridge.
'Wheee!' said Topsy as they trundled it down the other side.

There was a little shop on the platform. Topsy and Tim chose some comics to look at on the journey.

A lot of people were waiting for
the train. At last a loudspeaker told
them it would soon arrive.

'Here's our train,' shouted Topsy.
'I saw it first,' said Tim.
It was quite a scramble to get
on to the train.

'Stay close to me and mind the gap,'
said Mummy.

There was quite a squash inside the
train, too, but Mummy found some
empty seats.
'Sit by that window, Tim,' she said.
'You sit this side, Topsy.'

'That isn't Topsy,' said Tim.
They had got the wrong little girl,
but her mummy was not far behind.
'I think I've got your little girl,'
she said to Mummy.

Soon the train was rushing through
the countryside.
'I can see a pony,' said Topsy.
'I can see some cows,' said Tim.

The little girl's name was Clare.
She saw some cars waiting at a
level crossing for the train to pass.
Topsy and Tim and Clare waved
to the drivers.

'Tickets, please,' said a friendly voice. It was the ticket inspector. He had come to clip their tickets.

'Are you off on your holidays?' he asked.

'We're going to stay with our granny,' said Topsy and Tim.

'Can I come, too?' asked the ticket inspector, but he was only joking.

He made a neat hole with his clippers
in each of their tickets.

'Are we nearly there?' asked Tim.
'Not yet,' said Mummy.
The door at the end of the carriage opened and a lady pushed a rattly trolley towards them. It was filled with things to eat and drink.

'Would you both like a sandwich?'
asked Mummy.
'I want a ham sandwich,' said Tim.
'A cheese sandwich, please,' said
Topsy. They both had some orange
juice and Mummy had a cup of coffee.

Suddenly the train rushed into a long, dark tunnel.

It made the carriage look gloomy
and strange.
'Oooer!' said Topsy.
'My ears feel funny,' said Tim.
'Drink some orange juice,' said
Mummy. 'Then they'll feel better.'

At last the train stopped at Granny's
station. 'There's Granny!' shouted
Topsy and Tim.
Granny was very pleased to see them.
'Did you enjoy your train ride?'
she asked.
'Yes, we did,' said Topsy and Tim,
and they told Granny all about it
on the way to her home.

Topsy + Tim

go to hospital

Tim was going to hospital.
He had fallen out of a tree
and bumped his head.
Topsy and Mummy helped Tim
to pack the things he would need
in hospital.

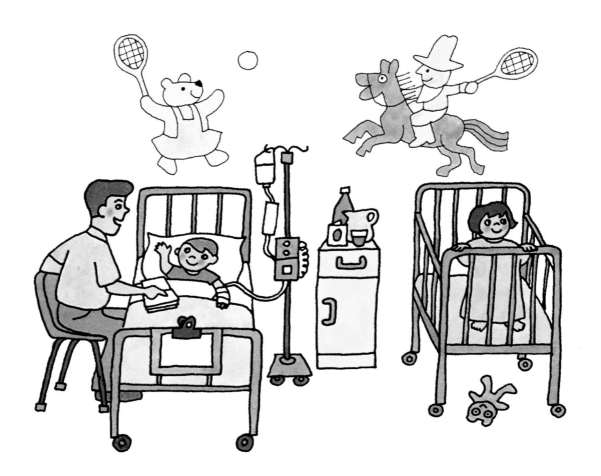

The hospital was very big,
with bedrooms called wards.
One ward had funny pictures
on the walls.
'This must be the children's ward,'
said Mummy.
A nurse called Sister helped Tim
put his things away in his own
special locker.

'The porter will take you to be
photographed in a minute,' said Sister.
'It will be an X-ray photograph—
the kind that shows what you
look like inside.'

The porter came,
pushing a big
wheelchair for Tim
to sit in.
'Can Mummy come
too?' asked Tim.
'Of course she can,'
said Sister.

It was a long way to the X-ray room.
Tim enjoyed his wheelchair ride.

He saw another porter pushing a
little girl along. She waved to Tim
as they passed.

The lady who worked the X-ray camera stood behind a screen. She could see Tim through a little window.

Mummy stayed with Tim but she
had to wear a special apron.
The X-ray photograph was soon taken.

After lunch, the children went to bed.
Mummy tucked Tim in.
'Now I must go home to look after
Topsy,' she said. 'But don't worry,
I'll soon be back.'

'Bring Topsy with you,' said Tim.
'I will,' said Mummy, but Tim
didn't hear. He was already
fast asleep.

Topsy brought her best jigsaw puzzle
when she came to see Tim in hospital.
She thought he would like to play
with it in bed.

Tim was not in bed. He was playing with the other children.

He took Topsy to meet his new friends.

On the way home, Topsy told Mummy
she had a pain—but she was not sure
where it was. Mummy did not
believe her.
'I want to go to hospital too,'
said Topsy.

'Cheer up, Topsy,' said Dad, when
he came home from work. 'I've brought
a surprise present for you.'

The surprise present was a medical set with a syringe, a stethoscope and a thermometer.

When Topsy came home from school
next day, she found Tim waiting
for her.
'Mummy brought me home,' said Tim.
'My head's all right now.'

Soon every toy in the house was in
Topsy and Tim's children's hospital.

Topsy + Tim

go to the dentist

It was time for Topsy and Tim
to visit the dentist. Mummy took
them to see Mrs Berry, the dentist
at the Health Centre. They sat in
the waiting room and read comics.

The dentist's door opened and out
came Josie Miller and her mummy.
Josie smiled at Topsy and Tim.
'I've got to wear a brace on
my teeth,' she said.
'Why?' asked Topsy.
'To make my teeth grow straight,'
said Josie.
'Mrs Berry is ready to see you now,
Topsy and Tim,' said the nurse.

'Hello twins,' said Mrs Berry.
'Your surgery smells funny!' said Topsy.
'It's a nice clean smell,' said Mummy.

'Who wants to go first?' said Mrs Berry.
'ME!' said Tim. He climbed into
the dentist's chair.
Mrs Berry pressed a button
and the chair tilted back.
Tim felt like a rocket pilot.
Mrs Berry put a disposable mask
over her nose and mouth.
'What's that for?' asked Tim.
'So that I don't breathe over you,'
said Mrs Berry.

'Open wide and let me see your teeth,'
said Mrs Berry.
Tim opened his mouth as wide as he could.
'This small mirror will help me
look for holes in Tim's teeth,'
said Mrs Berry. 'Little holes can
turn into big holes and big holes
can turn into toothache!'

There were no little holes in Tim's teeth.

'Your turn now, Topsy,' said Mrs Berry.
She found a little hole in one of
Topsy's teeth.
'I'll clean that hole and put
a filling in it,' said Mrs Berry.
'It will stop pieces of food getting
in and turning nasty.'
First Mrs Berry hung a sucking
tube in Topsy's mouth.
'That's to stop you dribbling,'
she said. The tube made
funny sucking noises.
Then she used her whizzy
drill to clean out the hole
in Topsy's tooth.

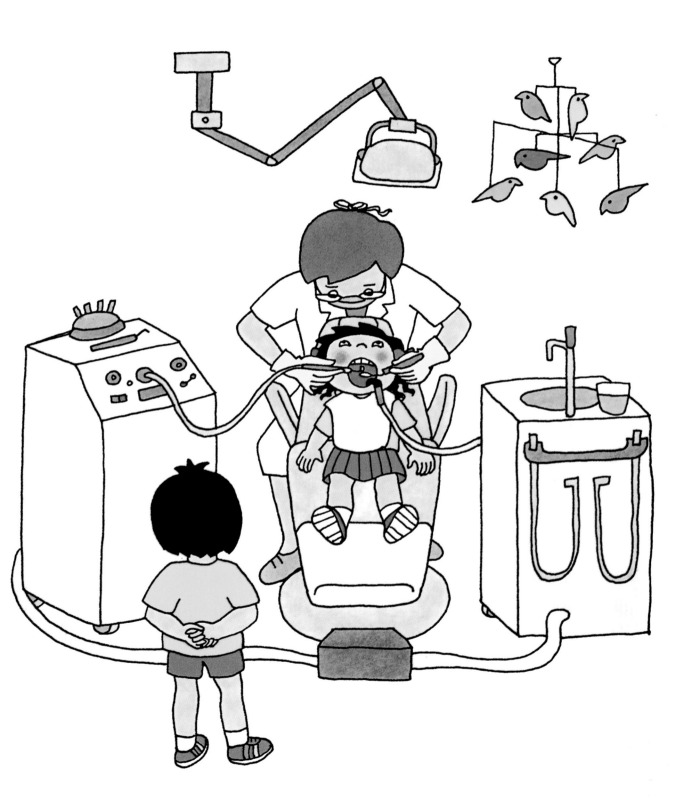

The nurse gave Topsy a glass
of pink water to rinse her mouth.
Then Mrs Berry dried the hole
with a little air blower,
so that the filling would stick
tight inside it.

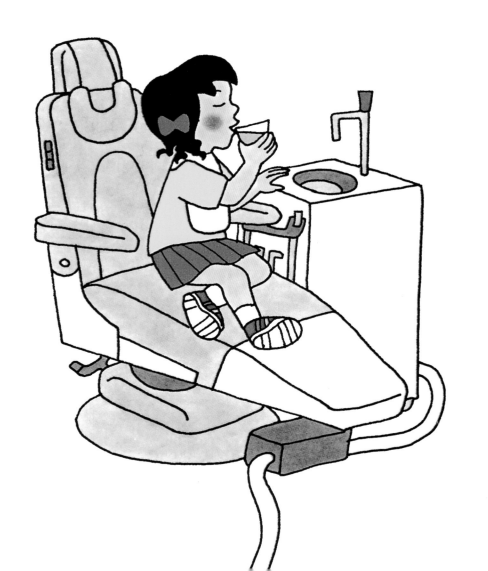

The nurse mixed a tiny bit of
silver filling. Tim watched her.
'That's Topsy's filling,' she said.

Mrs Berry pushed the silver filling into the hole in Topsy's tooth. She pressed it down and made it perfectly smooth.

'There! Good as new!' said Mrs Berry.
'Did it hurt?' asked Tim.
'The drill was noisy,' said Topsy.
'But it didn't hurt.'

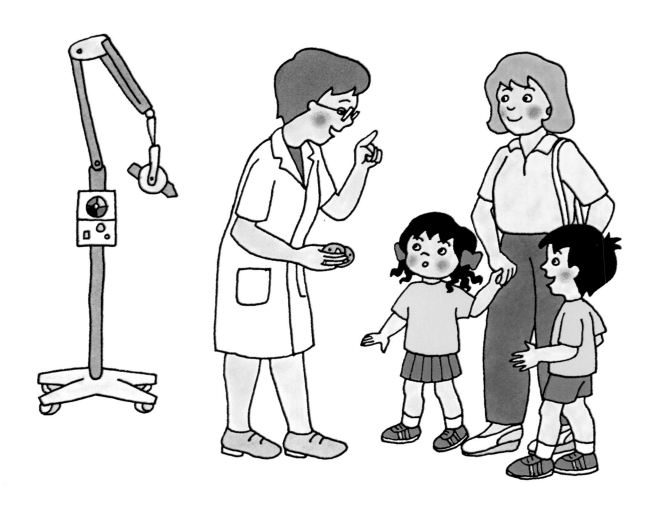

'You've both got good teeth,' said
Mrs Berry. 'Keep them that way.
Eat lots of different foods but remember,
sweet foods can hurt your teeth,
so don't eat them too often.

Never forget to clean your teeth
in the morning and at bedtime
and don't eat or drink in bed.'
'Not even water?' said Tim.
'Only water,' said Mrs Berry.
'Sweet drinks can hurt your teeth
as much as sweet food.'
Mrs Berry gave Topsy and Tim
a badge each to remind them
to look after their teeth.
'Come back and see me soon,' she said.

Before they went home the receptionist
wrote down the date of their next visit.
A little boy came into the waiting
room with his mummy. He was trying
not to cry.
'It's Tony Welch,' said Topsy.

'What's the matter, Tony?' asked Tim.
'I've got toothache,' sniffed Tony.
'He eats too many sweets,' said
Tony's mum.
'Never mind,' said Topsy. 'Mrs Berry
will make it better.'

On the way home they passed a sweet shop.
'I would like some sweets,' said Topsy,
'but I don't want toothache like Tony.'

'There are other nice things that are better for you,' said Mummy. She bought them lovely crunchy apples from the greengrocer.

Then they went to the chemist
to buy new toothbrushes.
The chemist told them about
disclosing tablets.
'Just chew half a tablet, then
rinse your mouth with water,'
he explained. 'The parts of your
teeth that most need cleaning
will turn pink.'

'We'd look funny going to school
with pink teeth,' said Tim.
The chemist laughed. 'You
clean away the pink bits with
your new toothbrushes,' he said.
'When there is no pink left,
you know your teeth are clean.'

As soon as they got home Topsy
and Tim tried out their new
toothbrushes.
'Mrs Berry won't find any holes
in our teeth next visit,' said
Topsy to Tim.